Boogie Knights

words by Lisa Wheeler   *pictures by* Mark Siegel

A Richard Jackson Book * Atheneum Books for Young Readers * new york • london • toronto • sydney

It is midnight,

and the moonlight's
shining down upon the moors
while the rascals
in the castle
jangle chains and rattle doors.

Seven zzzzing—
never seeing—
creeps are creeping through the hall,
down the stairway,
making their way
to the Madcap Monster Ball!

Werewolves hustle.

Zombies bustle
from their coffins, crypts, and vaults.

Mummies mamba.

Serpents samba.

Wicked witches do the waltz.

While upstairs, unawares . . .

In their chamber,
dreaming danger,
these six knights don't hear a thing.

Standing, posing—
knights are dozing,
then the banshee
starts to sing!

The windows crack.

The banshee nears.

Shrieks fill the air.

Sir Veillance hears.

He heads downstairs.
He just can't wait.
(He's eager to investigate.)
Behind the couch . . .

he cranes his neck.
His living room—
a discothèque? . . .

Monsters mashing!

Bogeys bashing!

Jesters jive and jump.

Go-go goblins—
bouncin', bobbin'—
teach that knight to . . .
Bump!

TAP
TAP
TAP

While upstairs, unawares . . .

Five brothers snooze
while one hears clues—
a monstrous melody.
Midst howls and cries
goes big **Sir Prize.**

"SHH"

"They're not expecting me."

Sir **Prize** jumps up.
He calls out

BOO!

. . . but soon that knight is dancing too.

While upstairs, unawares . . .

"It's getting late,"
tough **Sir Loin** states.

"Our honor is at stake."

He heads right down

with wide **Sir Round** . . .

and now *they* shimmy-shake.

Wizards wiggle!
Ghostlings giggle!

Demons do their thing.

Gremlins groovin'!
Vampires movin'!
See that hunchback swing!

While upstairs, unawares . . .

Three knights stand tall
along the wall,
their tarnished armor rusting.

TCHoo!!

A courtly sneeze—
"My allergies! These tapestries need dusting."

OUCH!

Then smooth **Sir Cumference**
tiptoes down
in stocking feet
he circles 'round.

He bends his knees.

He makes a fist.

He hears the beat. . . .

He does the twist!

Just two remain
and it is plain

they're running

out of time. . . .

And that's not all—
out in the hall,
a monster conga line!

Forced, **Sir Ender**
just gives in.

Lone **Sir Vivor**
(that's his twin)
feels the music
in his soul,
kicks up his heels . . .

"Let's rock 'n' roll!"

Toes are tappin'.
Knights are rappin'.

Feel the bass drum boom.

Knees are knockin'!
Knights are rockin'!

Give those guys some room!

Long past midnight
and the moonlight's
fading fast and nearly gone.
Seven brothers
and the others
party on into the dawn.

Shiny faces
take their places,
standing weary in the hall.
Seven sleepers
close their peepers—
dream of next year's monster's ball.

Nighty knight!

For Andy, Jen, Mia, and Ava Haroulakis
—L.W.

For Ann Bobco
—M.S.

Atheneum Books for Young Readers
An imprint of Simon & Schuster Children's Publishing Division
1230 Avenue of the Americas, New York, New York 10020
Text copyright © 2008 by Lisa Wheeler * Illustrations copyright © 2008 by Mark Siegel
All rights reserved, including the right of reproduction in whole or in part in any form.
Book design by Mark Siegel, Ann Bobco, and Michael McCartney
The text for this book is set in Regula Antiqua.
The illustrations for this book are rendered in charcoal, pierre noire pencil, and in Photoshop.
Manufactured in China
First Edition
2 4 6 8 10 9 7 5 3 1
Library of Congress Cataloging-in-Publication Data
Wheeler, Lisa, 1963–
Boogie knights / Lisa Wheeler ; illustrated by Mark Siegel. — 1st ed.
p.   cm.
"A Richard Jackson book."
Summary: When the knights of the castle are awakened by the noise from
the Madcap Monster Ball, they decide to join the party.
ISBN 13: 978-0-689-87639-4
ISBN-10: 0 689 87639 4
[1. Monsters—Fiction. 2. Knights and knighthood—Fiction. 3. Parties—Fiction. 4. Stories in rhyme.]
I. Siegel, Mark, 1967– ill. II. Title.
PZ8.3.W5668Bal 2008
[E]—dc22   2007024158